The adventures continue...

The Fred the Mouse™ series continues with these exciting stories:

Coming Soon...

FRED THE MOUSE™ Rescuing Freedom - Book Three
Coming Fall 2006

FRED THE MOUSE™ School Days - Book Four
Coming Spring 2007

FRED THE MOUSE™   Field of Geese - Book Five
Coming Fall 2007

Do you have your copy of
Fred The Mouse™ - The Adventures Begin?

Get your copy today at:
www.reesehaller.com
or
www.personalpowerpress.com

D1473090

ACKNOWLEDGMENTS

I would like to thank all the adults in my life who have been helping me reach my dream by supporting me with love and assistance. I thank my dad for taking me to

schools all around the country to talk about my love of writing and for helping me see that I don't have to wait until I'm older to change the world. I thank my mom for continuing to treat me like a kid and reading to me every night and for showing me how much fun the world can be. I thank my brother, Parker, for his excitement over the first Fred book and for encouraging me to hurry-up and write the second. I thank Mrs. Galsterer, for once again creating the sketches of Fred and his friends exactly the way I pictured them in my mind. Lastly, Chick (Moorman), thanks for being my editor. I appreciate your comments and the gentle way you made suggestions.

I appreciate you all.

FRED
The Mouse™
Making Friends

Book Two

Written by Reese Haller

Illustrated by Lynne Galsterer

PERSONAL POWER PRESS Inc.

Fred The Mouse™
Making Friends
Book Two

© 2006 by Reese Haller and Personal Power Press

Library of Congress Catalogue Card Number
2006900142

ISBN - 13: 978-0-9772321-0-9
ISBN - 10: 0-9772321-0-7

Printed in the United States of America

Personal Power Press, Inc.
P.O. Box 547
Merrill, MI 48637

Cover Design
Foster & Foster, Inc.
www.fostercovers.com

Book Design
Connie Thompson, Graphics etcetera
connie2@lighthouse.net

MY MISSION

I want to touch the hearts and minds of millions of kids around the world and help them see that they don't have to wait until they are older to become who they want to be. They can start now. Through my presentations and book writing I hope to inspire kids everywhere to read and then write their own books. I plan on creating a library where all the books are written by kids for kids.

Visit Reese's Website: **www.reesehaller.com**

Meadow

Pond

Fred's new
home in the
barn

Human's
house

Samuel's
rock pile

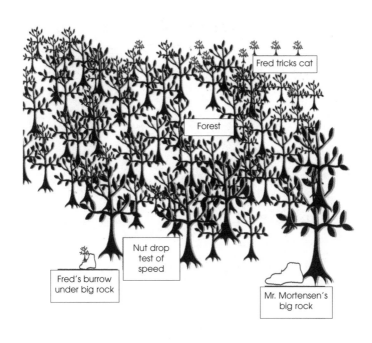

Fred tricks cat

Forest

Nut drop
test of
speed

Fred's burrow
under big rock

Mr. Mortensen's
big rock

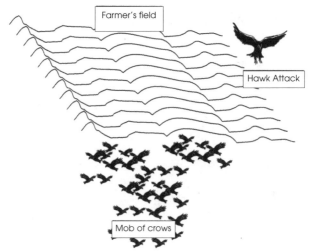

Farmer's field

Hawk Attack

Mob of crows

CONTENTS

Chapter 1

In Search of a Dream

 Fred looked over his shoulder at his mother as he scurried along the field's edge and out of his parent's sight. He was now on his own in search of the magical place he had dreamt about just a few hours ago. As Fred swiftly moved through the tall grass and wildflowers that grew at the edge of the field, he thought about his dream. In his dream he imagined a place where animals of all kinds lived together in harmony. His colorful dream, full of images of a dog, a cat, birds, and a snake, also included a feeling of comfort and peace. Fred wanted to find this place, and he made a promise to himself to keep looking until he did.

The path he now walked was a familiar one. It led towards the home where Fred and his nine sisters were born. A big green monster had destroyed that home when Fred was just learning to scurry and scamper. With their home completely demolished, the family had left the field and created a new dwelling under a rock at the edge of the woods where they now lived.

The surroundings smelled familiar, but did not look the same. What was once a field of corn was now a meadow of wild-flowers and tall grass. Fred spotted a tall clump of grass surrounding a single pink flower. He walked around the clump of grass. He could smell the rich scent of the flower. Fred closed his eyes and he breathed in deeply. His tummy lurched and tightened, the scent in the air changed, and, without thinking, Fred dove to the ground and scurried to the nearest tuft of grass. When he looked up, he could see a huge owl diving out of the sky directly towards him. The owl's talons were stretched forward and glistening in the early morning light. With nowhere to hide, Fred darted to the left, and the owl turned sharply in mid-air. A burst of speed came upon Fred as he immediately changed directions and in a flash was running straight at the owl's outstretched talons. Catching the owl by surprise, Fred ran directly under a talon as it closed seconds too late. The owl turned just in time to see a glimpse of Fred disappearing into an early morning fog gathered around a thicket of wildflowers.

Growing in the middle of the wildflowers
was a small tree with a trunk thinner than
Fred's body. He stopped to catch his
breath and noticed the fog that had settled
around him. He decided to wait for the
owl to give up his hunt and for the morn-

ing to give way to the brightness of the day. He hid in the protection of the fog until the warmth of the sun drew the fog from the air.

An hour had passed before the fog lifted and Fred began to see his surroundings more clearly. Gathered around him were tall green vines and pink flowers reaching to the top of a small, thin tree. The sky was a bright powder blue without a cloud to be seen, or an owl. Fred figured that the owl had given up his hunt and retreated to the woods for a day of rest. With a quick sniff of the air and another slow glance across the sky, Fred shimmied up the side of the small tree.

The tiny tree was surprisingly strong for its size, and Fred was able to climb higher than the wildflowers. He stopped climbing as the slender tree trunk began to bend from his weight. From his position, Fred could see across the field. As he looked in the direction of where he thought his home was once located, he saw something that looked like a mountain. Fred could not remember living by a mountain, and his parents had never mentioned any mountains in this area. Fred was curious, and he decided to use the light of the day to embark on an exciting adventure. This time he would create a mountain-climbing adventure.

Fred slid down the tiny tree and scurried off in the direction of the mountain. He began quietly singing the scurry and scamper song that his father had taught him.

First you put your nose up,
Sniff, sniff.
Then you put your ears out,
Twitch, twitch.
Open up your eyes,
Blink, blink.
Then we scurry and scamper.

Fred stopped from time to time to check his feelings and to double-check the sky to make sure the owl did not return for an afternoon snack. He found it easy to weave along the ground through the meadow, and reached the base of the mountain in short time. The familiar smell of home was stronger now, and Fred realized that the mountain was close to where his home had once been.

The mountain was easy to climb. It was

not made of dirt or rock, and within minutes Fred stood at the top. He now realized that this was not a mountain at all but a neatly stacked pile of smooth wood. He moved to the edge and looked out across the field. Being up so high enabled him to see further than ever before. He could almost see all the way back to his

parents' home beneath the big rock. He could see the field where the final exam took place and where he had out smarted the mob of crows just a few short days ago. In the opposite direction, he saw another mound that looked like a pile of rocks. Fred decided to head to the rocks in the distance and examine the pile more closely. He scurried down the lumber pile and scampered across the field in the direction of the next possible mountain.

Chapter 2

Samuel

Slightly out of breath, Fred stood at the base of a huge pile of rocks. The rocks reached into the sky and seemed to touch the clouds. As Fred squinted to see the top of the pile, he pondered how to find a way to the peak. A clear path was not easily seen, and the rocks appeared sharp and jagged. Fred closed his eyes and listened to his inner thoughts. He took a deep breath and searched for his inner feelings. A tingle started in his tummy and spiraled through his body, sending waves of heat to the top of his head and the tip of his tail. What he sensed was not danger or fear but excitement and thrill. Something seemed to be urging him to climb.

Fred opened his eyes and again looked up at the gigantic mound that lay before him. He walked around the base of the pile, looking for a place to begin his climb. A rock that looked like the stump of a tree caught his eye. Having scaled a tree to trick a cat when trapped in the woods during scurry and scamper class, Fred decided this would be a perfect spot to begin.

He moved up the first few rocks rather easily. His confidence began to build with every step he took. He jumped from rock to rock and soon found himself half way up the pile. He stopped to look out across the field. He could see further than ever before. His curiosity grew as he wondered what it would be like at the top of the pile.

The rocks were at a much steeper angle on the second half of the pile. That made the climbing much more challenging. Fred leaped to reach the bottom edge of a jagged rock and hoisted himself up slowly. His front paws held tight while his back paws searched for a place to grip and support his weight. Fred's right paw slipped, and his feet gave way. He hung over the edge, dangling by only one paw. Just as his left paw let loose of the rock, his feet found a small ridge in the rock and he pushed himself to the next ledge.

The top of this rock was round, smooth, and slippery. Fred had difficulty standing on it. To reach the next rock, Fred would have to cross a large crack twice the size of

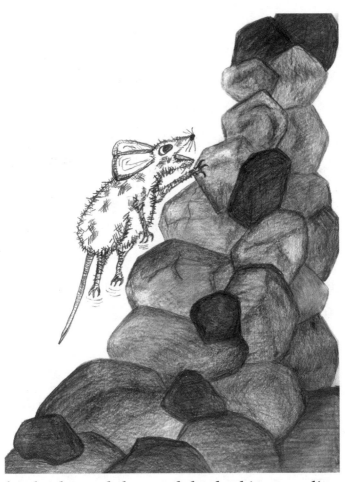

his body, and that rock looked just as slippery as the one he was currently standing
on. A small pebble slid out from under
Fred's back foot and fell into the crack. It

disappeared into the darkness, and Fred never heard it hit the bottom. He looked into the large crack; inside was a vast chamber of darkness. He tipped his head and looked at the boulder above him on the other side of the crack. He coiled his body and with all his strength leaped for the rock overhead. He caught a small rough edge of the mostly smooth slab and, with all his strength, hoisted himself up and onto it.

Now there were only two rocks to go and Fred would be standing on the top of the pile. Two more obstacles stood between him and his goal. He was two rocks away from a great feeling of accomplishment.

Without hesitation Fred jumped to the next rock and quickly onto the top rock.

He made it! He stood up on his hind legs with excitement, as if to celebrate his accomplishment. At that precise moment, the top rock shifted. Fred lost his balance and fell to the edge. The huge rock began to slide and slowly roll from the top position.

Fred had to make an instantaneous decision: to hold on to the rock and possibly be crushed as it rolled, or to let go and fall out of control. In a split second, Fred let go and began to tumble head over tail. He vanished head first into the darkness of the crack that he had jumped earlier. He bounced off a sharp rock and continued to fall. As he fell, all Fred could think of was the hard landing that awaited him. Within seconds Fred hit the ground, or what he thought was the ground. His landing was surprisingly soft. Fred sat up and turned to see two yellow eyes glowing at him in the darkness. He froze.

"H-Hello," stammered Fred.

"Hello," replied the creature.

"Who are you?" asked Fred, now working hard to calm himself.

A thin sliver of light was shining through a crack between the rocks. The creature moved into the light. Fred could now see what he had landed on. A snake! The snake was mostly black, with two yellow stripes running down its back. Fred moved closer to the snake.

"Interesting," commented the snake.

"When you s-s-saw what I was-s-s, you came closer instead of trying to run away. I would think a mous-s-se would be rather s-s-scared right now and attempt to run, yet you appear calm. Why is-s-s that?"

"I don't feel fear in my tummy. I feel gentleness and peace," replied Fred.

"Your feelings-s-s are accurate, young mouse. I don't eat meat. I am what others call a 'herbivore,' which is-s-s unusual for s-s-snakes, and yet s-s-somehow you s-s-sense this about me. I would like to talk with you more about this ability of yours. Do you care to s-s-share it with me?"

"Yes," replied Fred, "but can I have your name first?"

"Oh, I'm s-s-sorry. My name is S-S-Samuel S-S-S. S-S-Snake. And what is your name?"

"My name is Fred."

"Well, Fred, let's-s-s get out of here and enjoy the warmth of the s-s-sun."

Fred looked up at a small hole in the top of the pile. "How? We're a long way down. I don't think I can make it all the way up there."

"Follow me. We don't have to go up. We can go through the pile." Samuel slowly slithered towards a crack between two rocks at the base of the pile. Fred followed Samuel's smooth yellow stripes through the winding passageway. Samuel seemed to move with ease and grace around the sharp rocky edges. Ahead in the distance Fred began to see a small glimmer of light. As they inched closer, the light grew larger and the outside world came into sight.

Fred saw Samuel clearly for the first time when he reached the exit of the rock-pile

home. He was a thin snake about two feet long. His yellow stripes shimmered in the sunlight against his smooth, black scales.

Samuel spiraled his long body into a circle on top of a smooth flat rock in the direct sunlight. Fred joined him on the rock, and the two began to share stories about their families and their past.

Fred learned that Samuel's family had difficulty accepting his choice to not eat meat. His father told him that it was not natural for a snake to eat only plants and if he didn't start eating meat he would have to leave home. Samuel had left home when he was very young, and has been living by himself at the edge of this field for several years. He remembered spending an entire day watching the farmer pick the rocks out of the field and dump them into a pile. The pile later became his home.

Samuel learned that Fred had recently left home in search of a meadow with tall grass and pink flowers where a variety of animals lived in peace and harmony with one another. He also learned that Fred had recently become the only mouse in history to complete a test of scurry and scamper skills where he outsmarted and outmaneuvered a band of crows to return home safely.

It was the tickle in Fred's tummy and his ability to sense danger that Samuel was most interested in. Samuel was extremely wise about many things in the world, and he sought to understand Fred's unique ability. Fred explained the sensations he felt and how he learned to trust what those feelings told him.

Together, snake and mouse sat in the warm sun becoming close friends.

Chapter 3

First Flight

As the morning sun rose higher in the sky and its warmth grew stronger, a flurry of activity began to take place over by the pile of wood. Two-legged creatures, that which Samuel called "humans," had arrived with machines and tools. Fred had never seen a human before and he was amazed at the sight of them. They were so large and moved so quickly. Samuel warned Fred that, of all the creatures, these were the most dangerous, and that he needed to stay away from them.

The two friends watched as a massive structure was erected before their very eyes. In one day a huge "barn," as Samuel called it, appeared, and as the sun began to set, the humans left almost as fast as they had arrived.

The cool of the evening began to settle in and Samuel retreated to the comfort of his rock-pile home. Fred, on the other hand, decided to have a closer look at the new addition to the field.

The structure was enormous. He ran to the center and looked up. It felt like he was outside, yet he could not see the evening sky. Fred walked slowly from one end to the other, looking closely at every detail and stopping to smell the air. As he moved closer to one end, a familiar scent began to fill the air. Fred moved faster as the scent became stronger, and he quickly found himself standing in front of a large green door. He closed his eyes and sniffed. The scent was stronger to the right. He slid his feet slowly in that direction and sniffed again. This time he felt compelled to dig under the corner of the door that stood before him. The ground was soft, and Fred quickly appeared on the other side of the door.

This side of the door was much different than the other. Fred had to keep his belly close to the ground as he moved so he wouldn't bump his head. The space was much smaller, and he could touch the boards above him easily. Fred continued to move in the direction of the familiar smell. His tiny legs moved quickly as his heart began to race. Then he froze. He did not take another step. Fred realized what the scent was and where he was now standing. The powerful aroma filled Fred's body with memories of home. He was standing in the very spot where he was born. Fred sighed as he allowed the memories to flood his mind. He laid down, curled up in a small ball, and closed his eyes. Fred slowly drifted off to sleep and began to dream.

Fred woke to a familiar sound, the chirping of a bird. It was dark, and Fred quickly moved to the opening he had dug earlier. He popped his head out slowly and could see the light of day coming from across the huge structure. Remembering the song that his father had taught him about how to smell, listen, and look to make sure it was safe, Fred exited the hole slowly. He picked a position close to the entrance of his newfound hiding spot and watched closely. He could see a small bird swooping in and out of the large opening in the barn, holding twigs in its claws and beak. Several times the bird appeared, and almost as fast as it flew in, it flew out again. Fred marveled at the speed of this flying creature. He watched for almost an hour as the bird continued to come and go with great precision and determination.

Fred was waiting for the bird to return when he realized that several minutes had passed and the bird had not come back. This was unusual. The bird had been returning with great regularity. Curious, Fred moved closer. No bird. He stood at the large opening and looked out. No bird. He looked up at the sky and saw nothing but the glimmer of the morning sun as it came over the trees in the east. He looked back into the barn and then up to where the bird had been diligently working. There, at the peak, was a tiny nest beginning to take shape. Fred's curiosity surfaced, and he decided to sat-isfy it. He quickly scurried to a long board leaning against the wall in a nearby cor-ner.

The board was at a slant, and Fred easily climbed to the top. The board, however, did not reach the rafters that lead to the nest. Fred stood motionless atop the long board, surveying the situation. He wasn't willing to give up just yet. He wanted to see in that nest. He spotted a string dangling from a nearby rafter, and without giving it much thought, he jumped. He grasped the string with his front paws and immediately started climbing. Fred

loved climbing, and this was just like climbing the tree vines in the woods as he used to do with his sisters each morning before the start of school.

Fred quickly reached the rafter and scurried across its upper edge until he came to another rafter board jutting out at an angle. The board was at a much steeper angle, and Fred had to grip tightly on to its edges as he slowly inched his way to the top. When he reached the top, he could see the nest, but it was about 42 'mouse feet' away. Fred knew he could make the jump easily if he had a running start, but that was out of the question on this steep board.

After several minutes of thinking, Fred decided to move to the very edge of the board and leap with all his might for the nest. He counted silently in his head, "1 - 2 - 3," and shouted, "Jump." He took flight for a brief second and caught the bottom corner of the nest with his front paws. Fred slowly clawed his way up to the top of the nest. Exhausted and panting, he plopped into the nest.

Once Fred caught his breath, he looked around, and to his disappointment the nest was empty. He sat up and peered over the edge of the nest. It was a long way down. "Wow," said Fred, "If I had looked down earlier, I probably would not have attempted that jump."

"Yep, that was quite a leap you made, little mouse."

Fred whirled around, and there standing behind him on the edge of the nest was a bird. It was the very bird he had been watching for the past hour.

"I agree!" said another voice from behind Fred again.

Fred spun about, and there was what appeared to be the same bird behind him on the other side of the nest. He looked back and forth from side to side and quickly realized that there were actually two birds that looked exactly alike.

"Oh, there are two of you. That explains how you could fly in and out of the barn with new building material so fast. I thought I was seeing one bird working. I was, in fact, seeing two."

"We get that all the time," said the bird on the right.

"I'm Lou, and this is my partner, Lou," said the bird on the left.

"Just call us LouLou," chimed the bird on the right, "And who might you be?"

"Oh, I'm sorry. My name is Fred. I used to live here before this barn was built."

"Fred?" asked Lou. "Fred the Mouse, the Scurry and Scamper Champion?"

Startled, Fred replied quietly, "Yes, but how did you know that?"

"You're famous. Everyone around these parts has heard of the only mouse who has ever passed the scurry and scamper exam and outsmarted the crows."

"We heard about you a few days ago from a mob of crows just south of here. They took great pride in being able to capture the school mice every year, and now they're really furious about being out-smarted by you."

The two birds were now standing next to each other and taking turns finishing each other's sentences.

"We, however, are delighted and honored to meet you. Those crows always think they're the smartest creatures around. You, little mouse, are welcome in our nest any time."

Fred sat with Lou and Lou in the nest and listened to the two birds explain how they grew up together, became best of friends, and decided to leave home together. He listened to their many stories about traveling south each year and living in a variety of barns around the country. He learned that they are called "barn swallows" and that building nests in the peak of a barn is what they do best. On their flight north, following a winter down south, they noticed this barn being built and decided to take up residence in the new structure.

The morning passed quickly and Fred didn't realize that the afternoon sun was high in the sky until his stomach began to growl with hunger. "I'm getting hungry," said Fred. "Would you help me figure out a way back to that piece of wood? I'm a little worried about making that long leap across."

Lou looked at Lou and smiled as only a bird can. "We can get you down. No problem. Just climb on my back."

"What?" exclaimed Fred.

"Climb on, this will be fun."

Fred looked over the edge of the nest. "Are you sure I'm not too heavy?"

"I'm sure," said Lou calmly, "I've lifted heavier things than you hundreds of times. Climb on!"

Fred closed his eyes, took a smooth breath, and listened to his inner feelings. A calmness fell over him and he knew exactly what to do next. Without hesitation he opened his eyes, stepped forward, and climbed onto Lou's back. "I'm ready," he said confidently.

Lou spread his wings and pushed into flight. He fell for a brief second and Fred's stomach tickled with pleasure. "WHEEEEEEEEEE!" shouted Fred as bird and mouse zipped through the air. Lou zigged and zagged through the air as a mouse would scurry and scamper across the ground. He even performed a few loop-d-loops before landing softly on the ground.

"That was fantastic," exclaimed Fred, "My first flight!"

Lou alighted next to Lou on the ground and proclaimed, "What a performance. I'm sure there will be many more like that to come."

Chapter 4

The Walking Rock

 Fred and his new friends, Samuel, Lou, and Lou, spent the next couple of weeks laying in the sun and flying in the sky. Lou was right. Fred had many more flights on the back of Lou. They were becoming a smooth flight team, gliding together, gliding through the air with ease and grace.

Every morning Lou and Fred would fly through the air taking note of all the changes to the land below. In the afternoon Fred would lay on the rock pile with Samuel in the warm summer sun. Together they watched as the landscape around them changed before their very eyes. One particular change caught Fred's attention. It was a huge hole that the humans had dug right in the middle of the field. Fred planned on taking an adventure to the hole for a closer look.

Fred decided to leave early the next morning to venture across the field and explore the giant hole. That evening, as Fred packed a small bag of his favorite berries, a light rain began to fall. The light rain quickly turned into a heavy rain with flashes of lightening and loud crashes of thunder. Fred was dry in his home in the barn, but the thunder kept him awake most

of the night.

When the sun rose to begin the next day, it was shaded by dark clouds and sheets of rain with droplets almost the size of Fred. Peering out of the barn, Fred had second thoughts about his adventure to the giant hole. Lou and Lou flew down and sat next to Fred as the three friends watched the rain cover everything they saw. Fred decided to wait for the rain to end to begin his journey across the field.

On the second day of waiting, Samuel emerged from his rock pile and slow-ly moved across the water-soaked ground and into the barn. His home at the base of the rock pile had slowly filled with water from the constant rain and the ground's inability to absorb any more moisture. He decided to spend the next few days in the dry comforts of the barn with Fred and LouLou.

It was not until the middle of the third day that the rain finally stopped and the sun began to shine again. Fred was anxious to begin his journey, even though the ground was still very wet. Samuel convinced Fred to first fly over the area with Lou before venturing out.

Lou and Fred took flight in the direction of the planned adventure. Water was everywhere, and to their amazement the giant hole was gone. It was not a hole any more. The constant rain had filled the hole with water, and a large pond had formed.

Back at the barn, Fred and Lou explained to Samuel and Lou what they saw. Fred decided to wait for the land to dry and then trek to the water for a closer look.

The following day, the humans returned and continued working at a rapid pace on what Samuel called a "house." He said that soon humans would be moving in and taking over the barn, too.

The summer sun quickly dried the land,

 and within a few days Fred was back to preparing for his adventure to the huge

hole, which was now a pond. Again he packed a small bag of his favorite berries, this time heading across the field in the mid-day sun.

Fred was winding through the field grass towards the pond when his stomach tightened. He knew exactly what that feeling meant: trouble. He stopped moving and quickly made himself as flat and as close to the ground as possible. Just as Fred lowered his body, a hawk swooped overhead, just missing his flattened body. Fred knew he would not be as fortunate on the hawk's next pass. He had to get out of the middle of the field and the hawk's direct line of sight.

With his body flat to the ground and his ears sticking straight up, Fred listened carefully. His mind was racing with thoughts of what to do next. He knew that a hawk's wings made a noise as they cut through the air. An owl flew silently, but not a hawk. Fred waited for the familiar sound. His wait was not long. Seconds later, the swishing of a hawk's wings filled the air. Immediately, Fred threw his bag of berries in the air. A split-second distraction was all he needed to be off and running at top speed. The hawk was not fooled by the small bag of berries, but Fred was fast, faster than any mouse this hawk had ever seen.

Surprised by the speed of this tiny creature, the hawk found itself out of striking distance once again. But his meal was in plain sight, with no place to hide. He turned sharply, and easily spotted his prey in the middle of the field. The hawk tucked his wings and dove.

Fred was running as fast as ever. He was looking for something, anything, to hide behind or to crawl under. He could not remember seeing anything when he was flying with Lou that could help him now. His only hope was to scurry and scamper like never before.

A quick turn to the left revealed a clump of grass. "Maybe I can make it," thought Fred. He dove head first for the clump, just as the hawk approached with out-stretched talons. Fred's head hit something hard. The hawk's talons hit the same thing. It was not a soft clump of grass, it was a green rock. Fred laid motionless next to the green rock while the hawk returned to flying a tight circle overhead.

Several minutes passed while Fred lay quietly, trying to catch his breath. He could see the hawk circling above, waiting for him to move. Eventually, he would have to move. The hawk would patiently wait to strike again. But, Fred did not move, he kept very still. But to Fred's surprise, the stillness did not last. The rock began to move. Fred jumped to his feet. The hawk's eyes spotted the movement. The rock continued on. Looking closer, Fred noticed that the rock seemed to have legs. He quickly ran to the front of the rock. It stopped and the legs disappeared.

This time Fred looked closer and could see a face hiding inside the rock. "Hello," said Fred. "I won't hurt you. You can come out from under that rock."

Slowly a head began to appear, and Fred could see a mouth and two tiny eyes. "Where is that hawk? Is it still out there?" came a low, deep voice.

"Yes, circling overhead," replied Fred. "He's trying to get me, and you saved my life."

"I thought he was trying to get me. I was

just walking along when I felt this hard thud on my shell," commented the deep voice.

"Oh, that was probably my head, when I ran into you. I thought you were a clump of grass. Then I thought you were a rock. Hey, what are you, anyway?"

"I'm a turtle, young mouse, and my name is Mortequie. Most just call me Mort. But, let's get out of this field before that hawk figures out what to do next."

With that, four legs popped out of the rock-like creature, and Mort began to walk. "Which way is home for you, Fred?" asked Mort.

"I live over there in that barn," replied

Fred, as he motioned with his front paw.

"Stay close to my shell and we probably won't have any problem with that hawk."

Mortequie walked very slowly, and it took a long time to get across the field and back to the barn. The hawk finally gave up and went in search of food at a nearby field.

Back at the barn, Fred introduced his new friend, Mortequie, to Samuel and LouLou. Mortequie told the others how he had been living for several years in the ditch along the side of the road. He heard that recently a new pond had formed, and he was on an adventure to take a closer look when he ran into Fred, or Fred ran into him. For the rest of that day the five different creatures talked, and laughed, and shared tales of the past. They became close friends that day, even with their obvious differences.

Chapter 5

The Mob

 The summer grew hotter and the human's house was taking shape just as Samuel had predicted. Mortequie decided that the pond was a perfect spot for a new home. Fred flew with Lou and Lou out to the pond almost daily for a cool dip in the refreshing water. Cattails had begun to grow along the edge of the pond, and Mortequie found an area for his friends to play in the water and have protection from the hawk, who passed by every now and then just to see if he could catch someone not paying attention.

It had now been several weeks since Fred

had left home in search of his dream. He was sitting in the hot sun with Samuel one afternoon talking about his sisters when he remembered that tonight would be the night that all his mice friends would be re-taking the final exam. Fred was the only mouse who did not have to spend the summer at the Mouse Scurry and Scamper School practicing their skills in preparation for another final exam. He decided to take an afternoon nap and then have Lou give him a ride to the big rock under the tree where the final exam was to take place.

Just before sunset, Fred and Lou arrived at the massive oak tree on the far side of the woods. Lou alighted on the ground next to the big rock. Atop the rock sat Mr. Mortensen with his eyes closed. Without looking up or even opening his eyes, Mr. Mortensen spoke, "Fred, have you come to oversee the final exam?"

"Yes, can we stay and watch?" asked Fred.

"You may. Please have your barn swallow friend escort you to those trees behind you, and remember to remain out of sight," replied Mr. Mortensen as he

motioned with his walking stick.

Lou flapped his wings twice and the two were quickly off the ground and zipping towards the trees. The closer they got to the trees the tighter Fred's stomach became. "Stop!" shouted Fred, "Turn around!" But before Lou could change directions, they found themselves in the midst of a clump of trees with every branch covered by large black birds. Lou remained calm and swooped to the right. He took a perch on a branch next to a particularly large crow. "Hello," said Lou casually.

"Hello," replied the crow, staring intently at Fred as if in a trance. He continued, "Do I know you, mouse?"

Fred began to stutter, "I ... I ... I don't think so."

"Tell him your name," interrupted Lou.

"M ... m ... my name is Fred," Fred said quietly.

"Fred? Fred the Champion? Hey, everybody!" shouted the crow, "We have greatness among us! This is Fred the Champion!"

All the crows turned to look at Fred and began to caw.

"Quiet!" shouted the large bird, "You'll give our position away." He turned to Fred and continued, "Mortensen said you would come. We plan to redeem ourselves tonight. No mouse will escape our new plan." The large crow leaned closer to Fred and whispered, "We're going to attack before Mortensen gives the signal. That way they won't be expecting us and we can catch them all off guard." Speaking again in a normal voice, the crow continued, "It's a pleasure to meet you, Fred, even though you have given us a bad name. Oh, by the way, my name is Maggilicutty. Most just call me Maggie." With that, Maggie took flight and the mob followed.

Fred and Lou sat quietly on the edge of a branch high in the trees, watching the final exam unfold. Maggie and the mob of crows did just as Maggie had said. They attacked before the signal and redeemed themselves, once again capturing all the mice at the Scurry and Scamper School.

After the exam was completed and all the young mice had returned to their parents, Maggie returned to the branch where Fred and Lou were sitting. "Some of the other crows in my mob would love to meet you, Fred. Would you like to join us for a celebration back at our nest?"

Fred looked at Lou. "Go ahead," said Lou. "I'm going to head back for the night. Maggie can bring you home when you're ready."

"Sure, that would be easy. If a tiny barn swallow can carry you on his back, I can certainly do the same," chimed Maggie in a bragging voice.

Feeling comfortable in the presence of his new crow friend, Fred climbed onto Maggie's back, and off they flew.

Chapter 6

The Humans Arrive

 Fred was changing. He no longer enjoyed being awake at night, which is what most mice do. He liked the daytime and being with his friends, Samuel, Lou, Lou, Mortequie, and Maggie. During the day he would take long flights with Maggie or fast zigzag flights with Lou. He would swim in the pond with Mortequie or lounge in the sun with Samuel. Fred was giving up his nocturnal ways and finding enjoyment, peace, and comfort in the daylight hours.

The summer days also included increased action with the humans. The six friends,

following Samuel's strong suggestion, kept their distance and watched the humans' house take shape. The action reached a peak just as Fred settled in for an afternoon of sunning on the rocks with Samuel. Four trucks and three cars drove up and stopped right next to the house. People began moving everywhere.

71

"It has-s-s begun," commented Samuel.

"What's begun?" questioned Fred softly.

"The humans-s-s are moving in. They will be s-s-staying," replied Samuel in a low, gentle voice.

"Are you sure? We've seen lots of action at the house before and no one stayed."

"We will need to keep a close eye on the humans-s-s. They tend to not like mice or s-s-snakes."

"What about LouLou and Mortequie?" asked Fred in a worried voice.

"Mortequie will be fine as long as he stays clos-s-se to the pond. But LouLou could have s-s-some trouble if a cat arrives-s-s."

"I might have some trouble with a cat, too," blurted Fred.

Samuel slowly turned to Fred, and in a calm voice said, "Yes-s-s, some changes-s-s will have to take place here at the barn. But let's-s-s not get too far ahead of ourselves-s-s and worry about the unknown. Today, we s-s-shall enjoy the warmth of the s-s-sun and the opportunity to be in it." With that, Samuel hissed softly, closed his eyes, and turned towards the sun.

Fred, on the other hand, kept a close watch on the humans. He was looking for any sign of a cat.

The day slowly passed and the sun began

to settle in the sky. Samuel retreated to his cave under the rocks and Fred to his home under the room behind the green door in the barn. That night Fred had difficulty sleeping. He kept waking up thinking about a cat living in the barn and how everything would have to change.

The next morning began with shouts from Lou and Lou, "Fred, Fred, FRED! The humans are in the barn!"

Fred slowly peeked out from under the green door. He was careful to only stick his head out part of the way, just enough to see what was going on. Sure enough, the humans were in the barn, and they were building something on the outside of the barn. Fred waited for a chance to sneak out to survey the situation. As soon as the humans walked outside, he scurried out of his hole, along the wall, and out the back door of the barn. Lou and Lou alighted next to Fred on the ground. "They're putting up a fence," they said in unison. "Those big round things that look kind of like trees without the branches are called 'posts.' They stick them in the ground and then add thin boards between the posts to make a fence."

"What's that smell?" asked Fred, as he curled up his nose.

"Oh, that's tar," said the Lou on the right of Fred. The Lou on the left interrupted, "It's really sticky, keeps the bottom of the post dry when they put it in the ground." Together they said, "You get that stuff on you and it never comes off. It is dangerous stuff. Just stay away from it."

Fred nodded as he remained fixed on the humans' every movement. The three watched for about an hour until the humans stopped working and went back to the house. Fred and Lou decided to take flight and get a closer look. Once in the air, Fred and Lou could see a huge pile of posts and several already in the ground sticking straight up. They also spotted Fred's worst fear, a cat. It was much smaller than the cat Fred had encountered in the woods. Lou said that it looked like it was a baby cat, called a kitten, and that it was probably only about three or four months old.

They circled overhead and watched the kitten carefully. It was playing around the posts. Not paying attention to its surroundings, the kitten walked across a post that the humans had begun to tar but hadn't put in the ground yet. After several steps into the tar it stopped. The kitten couldn't move, its feet were stuck to the post. Tar covered its tail and both of its back legs. Struggling, the kitten began to cry and whine for help, but the humans could not hear its cry. Lou circled closer. "We have to help it," said Fred. "But how?" shouted Lou as they flew past.

"Turn around. I have an idea," yelled Fred. "Fly by again, and this time get as close as you can to the kitten."

Cries rang out from the kitten below as Lou quickly spun about in mid-air. The tiny barn swallow, with mouse aboard, gathered speed as it swooped down from the sky. Just as Lou reached the kitten, Fred jumped, hurling himself into the air. Fred's body slammed hard into the side of the kitten, and the two went somersaulting through the air. They landed with a thump in a soft tuft of green grass. Fred immediately stood up and prepared to run, but the ground beneath him began to shake as laughter filled the air. He looked down and noticed that he was standing

on the kitten, who was rumbling with joy. "That was exciting, little mouse. Thanks for saving me."

"You're welcome." replied Fred, as a peacefulness settled into his stomach. "My name is Fred. What's yours?"

"Uh, I don't know. The people just call me kitty."

"Well, how about we call you . . . Tar?" said Fred, as he jumped from the kitten onto the ground.

"That's okay with me," replied the kitten.

"Come on," said Fred, as he motioned to Tar. "Let's see if my friend Samuel has any ideas on how to get that tar off of you."

Fred offered a paw to Tar and helped him to his paws, and the two marched off in the direction of the rock pile, paw in paw.

Chapter 7

The Watchdog

Everyone got involved in helping Tar get as clean as possible. Lou and Lou brought berries from the edge of the woods to rub on the gooey tar clumps stuck on Tar's legs. Mortequie brought mud from the pond, and Samuel applied a mixture of mud, sand, and grass to the sticky spots. Maggie and his mob stopped by with bright green oak leaves from the big trees in the woods to wipe the tar away. It seemed that the tar became less sticky with each new approach tried, but nothing took it away completely. Treatment after treatment was tried, and no one knew for certain what to do next. What was certain was that Fred and the other creatures around the barn were becoming the best of friends.

Fred had a friend to swim with, a friend to fly on long trips with, a friend to zigzag and do loop-d-loops in the air with, a friend to sit and relax in the sun with, and now a friend to go on cross-country adventures with. Because of his many friends, Fred enjoyed the long summer days and all the adventures he created with them.

On one particular day, while Fred and Tar were on a cross-country adventure, Fred discovered that Tar could also sense the presence of danger.

The two companions had been on an

adventure to the far side of the pond, playing amongst the cattails and chasing butterflies through the field. They were having so much fun that the time slipped past quickly and twilight was upon them. The sun gave way to a reddish gray sky, and a glimmer of the evening's first star began to shine. Fred was preoccupied with the flight of a butterfly when his stomach lurched and a feeling of terror instantly filled his body. Simultaneously, a piercing pain from a talon pinched his back between his shoulders. He had not responded fast enough to his feelings, and he was quickly being lifted into the air by a silent flying owl.

Just as quickly as he felt himself being lifted into the sky, Fred felt himself spinning to the ground. Tar had sensed the presence of the owl, too, and as the owl struck and began to lift off, Tar leaped high into the air and caught the owl in mid-flight. The three, Fred, Tar, and the owl, came tumbling down to the ground in a ball of fur and feathers. The owl quickly collected himself and took flight. Tar jumped to his feet and frantically searched for Fred. Dazed by the attack, Fred lay motionless in the tall field grass. Immediately, Tar picked Fred up gently in his mouth and ran across the field. Knowing that Samuel would already be in his rock cave for the night and that Lou and Lou were out flying with Maggie and the mob, Tar headed straight for the human's house.

He reached the back door just as the humans were coming out, "Look, honey, the kitty caught a mouse. Good kitty," said one of the humans as he patted Tar on the head. The two humans, climbed into the family car and drove away. Tar made his way into the garage and ran towards the back corner. He laid Fred down on a soft fleece mat and went to get some water from a nearby bowl.

Several hours passed before Fred began to move. "Tar, get over here. He is moving," came a deep voice from high above. Fred looked up to see a large pile of rust-colored hair standing over him. Too sore to move from the pain in his shoulders, Fred remained still.

"Don't move," said a familiar voice as Tar came walking around the pile of hair. "This is Tiffany, the family's watchdog. You've been unconscious for a long time now. Tiffany has been laying with you to keep you warm."

"We were getting worried about you, Fred," said Tiffany in a deep, soft voice. "You should spend the night here with me. Tar says that you have a friend named Samuel that will know what to do if you're not better by morning."

Tiffany gently stepped over Fred and laid down next to him on the soft fleece. "The humans are coming up the driveway. Tuck yourself under my hair and remain still. I'll just lay here as I always do and they'll never notice you."

The humans pulled into the garage and got out of the car. Looking down at Tiffany laying quietly, one of them said, "Some watchdog. Never barked. Never even moved. It looks like we've got a watchdog that doesn't watch." They both laughed and proceeded into the house and closed the door behind them.

Fred stuck his head out from behind a tuft of hair. "What was that they were saying? I couldn't understand a single word."

"Oh, they were making fun of me. I love to just sleep and lay around. I don't know what they want from a Golden Retriever. Laying around is what we do best."

Tar quickly interjected, "Then you'll like Samuel. All he seems to do is lay around in the hot sun. We can take you to meet him tomorrow." After a brief glance at Fred, Tar added, "I think Fred needs his rest."

Fred laid back down next to Tiffany. Tar curled up next to the Golden Retriever and all three were fast asleep in minutes.

The next morning a gentle, soft paw nudged Fred awake. "How are you feeling today, my little friend?" whispered Tar.

"My neck is sore but the sharp pain between my shoulders is gone," replied Fred.

"While I'm still laying down, climb on my back and I will give you a ride to the barn. I can use the exercise. Besides, I want to meet this Samuel friend of yours," said Tiffany.

Tiffany tried to lay still, but Fred's tiny feet tickled as he walked up her back. Tiffany giggled a couple of times, and her back leg started to twitch. Fred crawled as best he could. His shoulder hurt a little more now that he was moving. He was glad that Tiffany was giving him a ride back to the barn.

Down at the barn, Tar had to yell several

times to finally get Samuel to respond. After a few minutes he emerged from under the rock pile to find a large dog, two barn swallows, a cat, and Fred staring him directly in the face.

"What's-s-s all the nois-s-se about? I'm a cold-blooded creature, you know, I need the warmth of the day to get me going. I'm not used to being up s-s-so . . ."

Tar interrupted Samuel in mid-sentence, "Fred's been hurt by an owl."

Samuel seemed to perk up immediately. "Let me take a clos-s-se look at him."

Tar guided Fred to Samuel's flat sun-bathing rock with a gentle paw. Samuel instructed Fred to lie very still as he looked over his wounds. "Hmmm, ahhh, ohhh," was all that Samuel said as he slowly slithered around Fred's body, closely inspecting his wounds with his sensitive tongue.

After several minutes, Samuel spoke. "Fred, you have a few s-s-small puncture holes-s-s on your neck and a nasty bruise on your s-s-shoulder. You're going to need plenty of rest and s-s-some healthy nuts-s-s and berries-s-s. You should be as good as new in a week or s-s-so."

A sigh of relief came from everyone at once. Then, as if someone had given them all a signal, they began talking at once. "We'll go get the berries," yelled Lou and Lou. "I'll get some soft grass," said Tar. "I can help transport Fred wherever he needs to go," chimed Tiffany.

Lou, Lou, and Tar were off in a flash. Tiffany laid down next to the flat rock and whispered softly to Fred, "This is one special group of friends you have here, Fred."

Fred smiled and nodded. "Yes it is. Yes it is."

Chapter 8

The Life of a Dream

The band of friends, including the addition of Tiffany, drew closer together as they all helped nurse Fred back to health. Samuel was correct; Fred was back to his normal self in just over a week. From that time on, Fred and his mismatched companions seemed to create a different adventure almost every day. Fred would join Maggie and the mob for adventures into the city. Lou and Fred would zip through the nearby forest dodging trees and bushes as they scurried and scampered through the sky. Mortequie created hours of water fun for Fred, Lou and Lou out by the pond. Tiffany would join Tar and Fred on their

cross-country adven-
tures in to the nearby
farmers' fields. Samuel
and Fred would meet
by the rocks after
every adventure to
talk about the day's
events and the happiness and excitement
it brought to those involved.

The humans came and went not paying
much attention to the band of creatures
that frequently gathered down by the
barn. The group of friends, eight in all
now, were all so very different, and yet
they had one thing in common. They each
accepted one another, even with their differences.

Dogs are not naturally friends with cats

and don't usually spend hours sun bathing with a snake. A mouse doesn't usually go on adventures with a cat or fly through the sky on the back of a crow. Barn swallows don't go swimming with a turtle and a mouse in the mid-day sun. Snakes are not usually vegetarians who consider a field mouse their best friend. But that is what makes this group of friends different from any other. They appeared mismatched on the surface, but

are matched together on the inside with their respect, understanding, and acceptance.

Fred came to a greater appreciation of what his world had become late one afternoon. The group of friends had gathered down by the rock pile as they frequently did when the summer evenings came to a close. Fred was the last to arrive, and when he came around the edge of the rock pile he gasped. There before him was the very same picture he had seen in his dream months ago.

Early in the spring, Fred had left home in search of a magical place where animals of all kinds lived together in harmony. He thought he would have to spend years searching for such a place. What he realized was that this magical place had come to life in his own backyard. What made this place possible was not found out in a field, or under a special tree. It was created by the attitudes of those who came together.

Fred slowly walked into the middle of his circle of friends. He looked at their gently, smiling faces and his heart filled with joy. His dream had come to life.

Mice
And others
From

FRED
The Mouse™
Making Friends

FRED: A young field mouse who is the mouse scurry and scamper champion from Book One. Not only is he the fastest mouse ever seen at the Mouse Scurry and Scamper School, he also has a unique ability of trusting his intuition.

SAMUEL: A wise old garter snake who lives under a rock pile near Fred's home.

LOU: A barn swallow that lives in a nest at the peak of the new barn that Fred calls home. He lives with his best friend, Lou.

LOU: Like his best friend, Lou, he too is a barn swallow. The two birds live in a nest at the peak of the new barn.

MORTEQUIE: A turtle that takes up residence in the newly formed pond.

MAGGIE: A large crow who is the leader of the "mob of crows."

TAR: A kitten who gets himself into a sticky mess.

TIFFANY: The human family's golden retriever watch dog.

MR. MORTENSEN: An old gray mouse, the principal at the Mouse Scurry and Scamper School.

Coming Soon!

FRED THE MOUSE™

Book Three

Rescuing Freedom

by Reese Haller

"Wow, what' s that smell?" asked Fred.

"That's the smell I was telling you about," replied Frank. "That's the wonderful smell that turned me from a field mouse into a house mouse."

"It sure does smell good. What is it?"

"The humans call it 'bacon and eggs.' I don't know what food up there is the bacon and what's the egg. I just know that there is always a lot of it on the floor when they're done," commented Frank, with a small bit of drool forming in the corner of his mouth.

"C'mon," interrupted Fred, "Let's go get some."

The two cousins were off in a flash. Together they scurried up the inside of the wall just under the kitchen and popped out of a tiny hole in the back of a cupboard full of pots and pans.

"Watch your step," whispered Frank. "Some of these pans tip easily and make a huge racket. It gets the humans all worked up."

Frank carefully weaved his way through the pans, with Fred close on his tail. Slowly the two mice lowered themselves down a space in the front of the cupboard and on to the kitchen floor.

"Stay close to the wall and follow me," whispered Frank, barely making a sound. Fred nodded a silent reply.

Along the base of the wall, they raced on their tiny legs as they both kept a close eye on every move the humans made. Not a single glance was made in their direction. The humans were fixed on eating. Arms and hands flew everywhere as the sound of forks scraping plates filled the air.

When they reached the other side of the room, Frank stopped. "We'll wait here in the corner."

Huddled in the corner under a collection of potted flowers on a tri-level stand, Fred could see the entire kitchen at a glance. Frank had obviously done this before. Not only could Fred see the humans and their strange eating behavior, but he could also see across the kitchen where they had just been a few minutes earlier, and into the next room.

Frank's eyes seemed to stay focused on the floor by the humans' feet. He appeared to be marking each tiny piece of food as it hit the ground and remember-ing its location. Fred, on the other hand, was drawn to the next room over. He didn't know why, but he felt like something was looking at him. Having learned to trust his inner feelings, he continued to scan the room with his eyes.

Several minutes passed, and then Fred gasped as a strange white creature appeared in the distance. "F-F-Frank, w-w-what's that?" whispered Fred with a hint of fear in his voice.

ABOUT THE
AUTHOR

Reese Haller

Reese is nine years old and a fourth grader at Kolb Elementary in Bay City, Michigan. He is considered the youngest published fiction author in America. He began writing short stories in kindergarten, where he was encouraged to take risks with his writing. He discovered his joy and passion in the third grade, where he blossomed as a writer.

While at the age of eight, before entering fourth grade, Reese wrote the first book in the <u>Fred the Mouse™ series: The Adventures Begin.</u> It has been nominated for a Michigan Notable Books Award and a Benjamin Franklin Award. For more information, visit Reese at <u>www.reesehaller.com.</u>

Reese is a regular presenter at elementary schools

across the country, where he lectures on the six traits of writing in a captivating 45-minute presentation. He has presented live to over 2,500 people in teacher in-services, keynote addresses, and numerous elementary classrooms discussing writing and publishing. In addition, Reese has been interviewed on television over a dozen times, reaching thousands with his message about writing and reading.

To assist teachers in the classroom he has also created an educational DVD on the traits of writing through the eyes of a young author. He has been nominated for a literacy award through the Michigan Reading Association for his contributions to the field of literacy.

Reese lives on an equine retirement and rescue ranch in Michigan with his parents and younger brother.

Reese's dad is an author of parenting books and a family therapist who lectures frequently on raising responsible, caring, confident children. He also writes a free monthly newsletter for parents and one for teachers. Visit him at www.thomashaller.com.

Reese's mom is a kindergarten teacher in the public schools, where she has taught for over 16 years. His brother Parker, age 6, enjoys rescuing bugs and playing the drums.

ABOUT THE ILLUSTRATOR

Lynne Galsterer

Lynne Galsterer is an artist whose creative interests include illustrating, picture and furniture painting, mosaic executing, and home decorating. Although holding a Bachelor of Arts degree in Medical Record Administration, she has always had a passion for the arts. Throughout the years she has volunteered in various art programs for the Saginaw Township school system. *Fred the Mouse™ The Adventures Begin* was the first book she illustrated.

Lynne was born in Saginaw, Michigan, and currently resides there with her husband, John. She has two daughters, Suzanne and Chelsea, both attending college, and two step-sons, John and Jeff.

 # Reese's Charity

I am donating a portion of the proceeds from the _Fred the Mouse_™ book series to **Healing Acres Equine Retirement Ranch, Inc.,** for the purpose of establishing a reading library at the ranch.

My goal is to create a library and maintain a reading program at **Healing Acres** where children have the opportunity to read with a horse or about a horse while they are visiting the ranch. I envision a place where children can read about how to care for a horse and then have a chance to touch, brush, feed, and even ride a real horse. I chose a wall in the barn that I want to turn into book shelves so people have a variety of reading choices about horses.

As a way to remember their experience, I will give to every visitor, young and old, a book about horses to take home.

I want every child to have the opportunity to experience the same joy I experience every day: the joy of reading and the joy of being with horses.

If you wish to make a donation beyond the purchase of this book, please visit: www.healingacres.com.

Thank you for helping me support my dream.

HOW TO INVITE REESE TO YOUR SCHOOL

Would you like Reese to come to your school for a Literacy Day?

It's easy. Just e-mail Reese at reese@reesehaller.com and ask about available dates for a Literacy Day.

You can also call Personal Power Press toll-free at 877-360-1477 and ask about scheduling Reese for a Literacy Day.

When you schedule a Literacy Day, your school receives:

• Reese for the entire day talking about his love of reading and writing.
• Signed copies of Fred the Mouse™ books
• A parent evening workshop where Reese and his dad give parents practical strategies and fun exercises that will inspire a love of writing in children.

INVITE REESE TODAY!!
www.reesehaller.com